Alice
the Tennis
Fairy

Special thanks to
Narinder Dhami

No part of this work may be reproduced, stored in a retrieval system, or transmitted in any form or by any means, electronic, mechanical, photocopying, recording, or otherwise, without written permission of the publisher. For information regarding permission, write to Rainbow Magic Limited c/o HIT Entertainment, 830 South Greenville Avenue, Allen, TX 75002-3320.

ISBN 978-0-545-20257-2

12 11 10 9 8 7 6 5 4 3 2 1   10 11 12 13 14 15/0

Printed in the U.S.A.   40

First Scholastic Printing, April 2010

Alice
the Tennis
Fairy

by Daisy Meadows

SCHOLASTIC INC.

New York   Toronto   London   Auckland

Sydney   Mexico City   New Delhi   Hong Kong

The
Fairyland
Palace

Fairyla

Parking Lot

Buses

Riding Stables

Cooke Soccer
Stadium

Basketball Courts

Soccer
Fields

Tippington
Town

REC CENTER

Swimming Pool

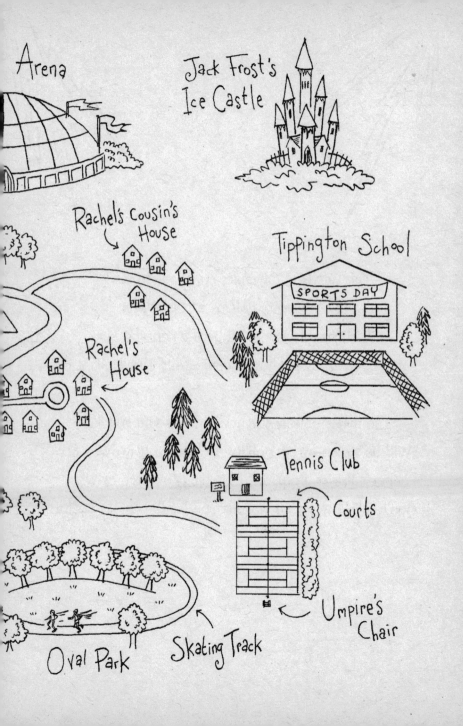

The Fairyland Olympics are about to start,

And my crafty goblins will take part.

We'll win this year, for I have a cunning plan.

I'll send my goblins to compete in Fairyland.

The magic objects that make sports safe and fun

Will be stolen by my goblins, to keep until we've won.

Sports Fairies, prepare to lose and to watch us win.

Goblins, follow my commands, and let the games begin!

Contents

Goblindon

"Isn't it a beautiful day, Kirsty?" Rachel
Walker said happily. She and her
best friend, Kirsty Tate, were walking
along a country path not far from the
Walkers' house, enjoying the sunshine.
"And it would be even better if we
could find another magic sports
object!"

"Yes!" Kirsty agreed. "The Fairyland Olympics start tomorrow, and Alice the Tennis Fairy's magic racket and Gemma the Gymnastics Fairy's magic hoop are still missing."

Rachel and Kirsty had promised to help their friends, the Sports Fairies, find their seven magic objects. Sports in both the human and the fairy worlds were not going well because Jack Frost and his goblins had stolen them.

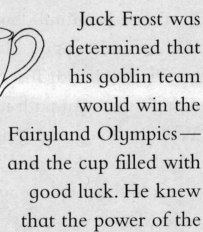

Jack Frost was determined that his goblin team would win the Fairyland Olympics— and the cup filled with good luck. He knew that the power of the

magic objects meant that anyone close
to one of them immediately became
fantastic at that particular sport. He
had sent his goblins into the human
world with each object, and told them
to practice for the games.

As the girls walked down the path,
Rachel suddenly noticed a strange sign
pinned to a tree. "Look at that,"
she remarked, pointing
it out to Kirsty.

The words on
the sign were
painted in bright
green and looked
very sloppy.
"*Goblindon*,"
Kirsty read aloud.
"And there's an

arrow with the words ENTRANCE TO
TIPPINGTON TENNIS CLUB—THIS WAY
written underneath it," she added.

"Oh no!" Rachel exclaimed.
"This has goblin mischief
written all over it! Mom
and I have played tennis
at that club once or twice,
and there are always lots
of people around. What if
the goblins are spotted
by someone?"

Kirsty looked worried. The girls knew
that nobody in the human world was
supposed to find out about Fairyland and
the goblins, fairies, and other creatures
that lived there.

"We have to find out what's going
on," Kirsty insisted. "If the goblins are at

the tennis club, they might have Alice's magic racket."

"Good thinking," Rachel agreed.

As the girls hurried off toward the tennis club entrance, they suddenly heard a loud voice coming from behind the bushes.

"Attention, goblins!" the voice announced. "I will now explain the rules of the tournament."

"The goblins are having a tennis tournament!" Rachel exclaimed. "Instead of being called Wimbledon, like the famous English tournament, it's called *Goblindon*!"

"There's only one rule," the goblin went on. "I'm the umpire in charge of this tournament, so what I say goes!"

He chuckled loudly, but Rachel and Kirsty could hear the sound of the other goblins muttering and complaining.

"How many of them *are* there?" Kirsty asked with a frown.

Rachel put a finger to her lips. "We're right next to the tennis courts," she whispered. "Let's look through the bushes."

The girls pushed some leaves aside
and peered through the hedge. Both
of them tried not to gasp out loud at
the scene in front of them. The
Tippington Tennis Club was full of
goblins!

Tennis Time

Kirsty and Rachel glanced at each
other in dismay. All the goblins were
wearing the proper white tennis shirts
and shorts, and they were stretching as
they got ready for the tournament.

"Luckily there don't seem to be any
humans around," Rachel murmured.

"Look, Rachel!" Kirsty said suddenly.

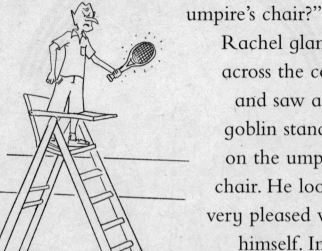

"See the goblin up there on the umpire's chair?"

Rachel glanced across the court and saw a big goblin standing on the umpire's chair. He looked very pleased with himself. In his hand, he held a pink tennis racket that shimmered in the sunlight.

"He has Alice's magic racket!" Rachel gasped.

"We *have to* try to get it back," Kirsty whispered.

"As you all know, the purpose of the Goblindon tournament is to perfect your tennis skills," the goblin umpire continued. "I want to see lots of powerful shots and fancy footwork! The Fairyland Olympics are coming up, and we want to beat those pesky fairies and win the cup full of good luck for Jack Frost!"

All the goblins cheered as the umpire waved the magic racket in the air.

"The winner of Goblindon will receive a special prize," the umpire announced. "He will become keeper of the magic racket for the day!"

The goblins cheered again as they stared longingly at the magic racket.

"They *all* want to win it!" Kirsty exclaimed.

"Yes, but I think the umpire would like to keep it for himself," Rachel pointed out, as the goblin umpire lovingly stroked the racket's pink handle. Then he nodded at two goblins standing on the sidelines.

"Bring out the ball machine!" he shouted.

The goblins began to push a giant ball machine onto one end of the court, right in front of the bushes where Kirsty and Rachel were standing. The girls jumped back quickly, afraid of being seen.

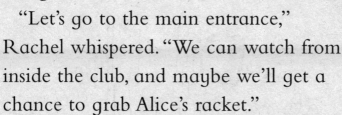

"Let's go to the main entrance," Rachel whispered. "We can watch from inside the club, and maybe we'll get a chance to grab Alice's racket."

The girls hurried down the path toward the gates of the tennis club. As they did, they heard the umpire talking

to the goblins. He explained that, in
the first round of the tournament, the
goblins would compete against the ball
machine.

"Any goblin who can return the
ball or dodge out of the way without
being hit, for a total of ten minutes, will
make it to the next round," the umpire
declared. "Any goblin hit by a ball will
be automatically disqualified."

The girls quickly ducked behind a tree
next to the club gates and peeked out.

They saw the umpire
goblin carefully put
the magic racket
down on his chair
and go over to the
ball machine. The

other goblins were all gathered on the
other side of the net.

"One, two, three, go!" the umpire
yelled, turning on the machine.

It immediately began firing tennis
balls at the waiting goblins. Some of the
goblins weren't ready. They didn't even
have the chance to lift their rackets
before they were hit by flying balls!

"That's not fair!" one of them
grumbled.

"You're out!" the umpire said sternly.

The goblins who had been hit

stomped grumpily off the court.
They began filling up the seats that
surrounded the court. Meanwhile,
the remaining goblins were
swatting and batting
the balls away.
They were barely
able to dodge
the balls they
couldn't hit.

"Look, Kirsty!"
Rachel nudged
her friend.
"What's the
umpire doing?"

The goblin umpire was grinning—
and it was a terribly mischievous grin!

As the girls watched, he flipped a
switch on the ball machine without

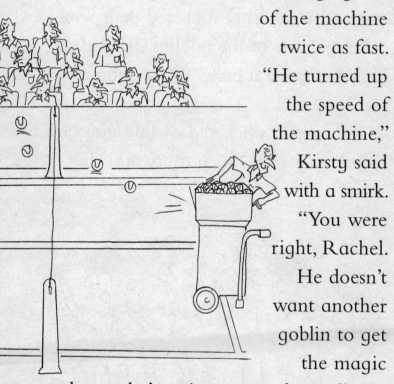

the other goblins noticing. Suddenly, the balls came flying out of the machine twice as fast. "He turned up the speed of the machine," Kirsty said with a smirk. "You were right, Rachel. He doesn't want another goblin to get the magic racket, so he's trying to get them all out."

The goblins on the other side of the net were now racing around the court,

whacking the super-fast balls here and there. But they hardly had time to hit one before another rocketed their way.

"Hey!" one of the goblins shouted as he sidestepped a ball. "What's going on?"

The umpire snickered. "I said you had to practice your fancy footwork!" he shouted back. Then he turned the speed up even higher!

Suddenly, one of the tennis balls spun away from the court and headed straight for the girls.

"Kirsty, look out!" Rachel cried.

But at that moment, something very strange happened. The ball instantly stopped in midair and floated right in front of the tree where the girls were hiding. A tiny fairy was sitting on top of it, smiling.

"It's Alice the Tennis Fairy!" Kirsty exclaimed.

Tickets, Please!

Alice lifted her pink visor up on her
forehead and waved at Rachel and
Kirsty. The fairy wore a white tennis
outfit and pink-and-white tennis shoes.

"Girls, I'm glad to see you," Alice said.
"I *really* need your help to get my magic
racket back."

"We know where your racket is,"

21

Kirsty replied. "It's on the umpire's chair."

Alice spun around and looked thrilled as she spotted her pink, sparkly racket. "How can we get it without being seen?" she asked eagerly. "Any ideas?"

"Maybe we should sneak into the club while everyone's watching the game," Rachel suggested.

They all looked at the court where the remaining goblins were still dashing back and forth.

"Good idea," Alice said.

The girls hurried through the gates. Alice flew next to them.

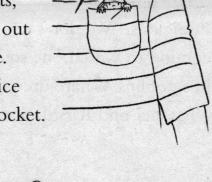

"I wonder where all the club members are," Rachel said, as they walked down the path toward the clubhouse. "It's amazing that nobody has seen the goblins yet!"

Alice smiled and pointed her wand at a poster on the clubhouse door. "That's why," she said. "There's a tournament today at Greendale Tennis Club."

"All the members must be playing there," Rachel agreed.

As the girls and Alice turned toward the courts, a goblin rushed out of the clubhouse. Immediately, Alice hid in Kirsty's pocket.

"Stop!" the goblin shouted. He was wearing a blue uniform and a cap with a bill. Alarmed, Rachel and Kirsty stopped as the goblin stared suspiciously at them.

"Where are you going?" he snapped.

"We came to watch the Goblindon tournament," Rachel replied bravely.

The goblin frowned, still looking suspicious. "We don't get many girls coming to watch," he said. "It's mostly just goblins. Where are your tickets?"

Rachel and Kirsty glanced nervously

at each other. They didn't have any
tickets! But just then Kirsty felt
something tingle in her pocket. She put
her hand inside and, to her surprise,
pulled out two large green tickets. Alice
was peeking out of the pocket, too,
smiling up at her.

"Here they are,"
Kirsty said cheerfully.
She handed the
tickets to the goblin.

The goblin stared
at the tickets while Rachel and Kirsty
tried to hide their smiles. Both girls knew
that Alice had made the tickets with her
magic—just in time.

"These do look real," the goblin
admitted, handing the tickets back.

"OK, you can go in."

Rachel and Kirsty rushed off,
breathing sighs of relief.

"Thanks, Alice," Kirsty said as the tiny
fairy fluttered out of her pocket. "Your
magic tickets worked perfectly."

Meanwhile, Rachel had come to
a stop at one of the clubhouse windows.

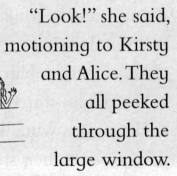

"Look!" she said,
motioning to Kirsty
and Alice. They
all peeked
through the
large window.

They could see a huge kitchen where
two goblins, wearing aprons and chefs'
hats, were spooning strawberries and
cream into lots of different bowls.

"It's the official food of Wimbledon,"

Rachel said, licking her lips. "They serve it at the tournament every year."

As the friends watched, the goblins loaded the bowls onto a cart and rolled it out of the clubhouse.

"Let's follow them and try to get the magic racket back while the goblins are stuffing themselves with strawberries and cream," Kirsty whispered.

Rachel and Alice nodded, and the friends snuck toward the tennis courts behind the cart.

Luckily, the goblins in the audience were too busy watching what was happening on the court to notice the girls. There were only five goblins left now, swinging at the balls flying from the machine.

"Look, my racket is still on the umpire's chair," Alice whispered. "I'm going to fly over and try to get it back."

"OK, but be quick, Alice," Kirsty said

nervously. "The ten minutes will be up soon."

Swiftly, Alice flew around the side of the court, keeping out of sight of the seated goblins.

Just then, the umpire blew his whistle. "The first round of Goblindon is now over!" he announced loudly.

The goblins broke into applause and immediately the umpire headed over to his chair.

Rachel and Kirsty stared at each other in horror. Alice was heading toward the chair, too. The goblin umpire could spot her at any moment!

"We have to distract him, Kirsty!" Rachel whispered. "But how?"

Double Distraction

Thinking quickly, Kirsty pulled her Goblindon ticket out of her skirt pocket. "Rachel, do you have a pen?" she asked urgently.

Rachel reached into her pockets. "Will a pencil do?" she asked, handing one to her friend.

Kirsty nodded, took the pencil, and

rushed across the court to the umpire goblin. He had almost reached his chair.

"May I please have your autograph?" she asked, holding out the pencil and her ticket. "I think you're the best umpire ever!"

"Oh, me too!" Rachel agreed, realizing what Kirsty was up to. She pulled out her own ticket. "Can I have your autograph, too?"

The goblin umpire looked very proud of himself. "Why, of course!" he replied with a wide smile.

As the goblin signed Kirsty's ticket,

Rachel saw Alice fly away from the umpire's chair. The fairy ducked behind a shrub, out of sight. Rachel sighed with relief. Kirsty's quick thinking had saved the day, but they still hadn't managed to get a hold of the magic racket.

Meanwhile, the umpire had finished signing autographs and was leaning back in his chair with Alice's racket on his lap. The girls moved to the side of the court and stood beside the cart of strawberries and cream. As they did, they saw one of the five winning goblins remove his white headband and replace it with a bright orange one.

"Hey, you!" the goblin umpire shouted immediately. "You're only allowed to wear white at Goblindon. You're disqualified!"

"But that's not fair!" the goblin protested.

"Please leave the court," the umpire insisted. "You are disqualified!"

"That's a rule at Wimbledon," Rachel explained. "The players only wear white."

The goblin sulked as he tore off his orange headband and stomped away.

"OK, the four remaining goblins will now play a doubles match," the umpire announced. "Then the winning pair will play each other in the final, and

the winner of that game will be the
Goblindon Champion!"

"Good work, girls," Alice whispered.
She flew out of the shrub and slipped
inside Kirsty's pocket as the doubles
match began. "Maybe we'll get a chance
to grab my racket during this game."

The goblins were speedy and skillful
tennis players, sending the ball flying
across the court at different angles.

"The goblins are playing really well," Rachel murmured.

"It's only because my magic racket is close by," Alice told her, as the smallest goblin dashed forward to return a low volley.

"Uh!" he grunted as he smashed the ball back across the court. Then, as it was returned to him, he hit it again and made another loud grunt.

One of the goblins on the other side of the net turned to the umpire. "He's distracting me with his grunting!" the goblin declared furiously.

The umpire pointed at the smallest goblin.

"No grunting allowed at Goblindon," he said sternly. "You're disqualified!"

"That's not fair!" the smallest goblin yelled, storming off the court as the audience laughed.

His doubles partner also looked annoyed. "I'm on my own now," he complained. "Two against one isn't fair."

"Very true," the umpire agreed. He glanced at the other doubles pair. "OK, one of you has to be disqualified, too, to even things up."

"Not me," declared one of the goblins, who had a very large green nose. "I'm a much better player than he is." He pointed at his partner.

"That's a lie!" his partner said, putting his hands on his hips. "You're not half as good as I am—your big nose keeps getting in the way of your shots."

"Ooh, you take that back!" the first goblin shouted angrily. He ran up to the second goblin, who turned and took off across the court. The first goblin chased after him, trying to bonk him on the head with his racket.

"This is the strangest tennis tournament I've ever seen!" Rachel laughed as she, Kirsty, and Alice watched in amazement.

"Stop!" shouted the umpire. He pointed at the first goblin. "You're disqualified for using your racket to hit a goblin. Rackets are for tennis balls!" he snapped. "Leave the court!"

"No!" the goblin said, pouting.

"You can't make me!"
The umpire jumped down
from the chair, leaving the
magic racket on the
seat. Rachel, Kirsty,
and Alice glanced
hopefully at
one another.
"This might be
our chance to grab
the racket if the
umpire has to chase the other goblin off
the court," Kirsty whispered.

"Off! Off! Off!" chanted the goblin crowd.
Muttering, the goblin player gave
up and stomped away. To the girls'
disappointment, the umpire climbed into
his chair, picked up the racket, and sat
down again.

"It's time for the Goblindon Final," the umpire announced, and the crowd broke into applause. "The champion will be the first goblin to win three games."

"We're not going to be able to grab the racket as long as the umpire's holding it," Rachel whispered.

"We'll have to wait until the tournament's over." Kirsty sighed.

"Yes, maybe we'll get a chance when they're celebrating at the end," Alice suggested.

The girls and Alice watched as the Goblindon Final began. Both goblins obviously wanted to win, and they raced around the court, straining and stretching to return each shot. The ball flew back and forth so fast it was a blur.

"This is going to be a very close match," Alice said anxiously. "I just hope it doesn't last too long!"

The third game began with a spectacular serve from one of the goblins. The other player struggled to make the return. The serving goblin then stumbled a little as he hit his shot. Grinning, the second goblin leaped forward and hit the ball. He aimed to send it to the far end of the court,

out of the other player's reach, but he mistimed his shot. The ball flew into the net, instead.

Immediately, he let out a shriek of rage. "I didn't mean to do that!" he yelled and threw his racket to the ground. "Someone moved the net!"

"You're disqualified for improper use of your racket," the umpire declared. "A racket should only be used for hitting things."

"I *did* hit something," the goblin shouted, dancing up and down in anger.

"I hit the ground!"

"That doesn't count." The umpire stared at him. "Off!"

As the goblin clomped off the court, his opponent raised his arm in victory. "I won!" he shouted. "I get to be the keeper of the magic racket!"

The umpire looked down at Alice's racket and frowned.

"Look, the umpire doesn't want to give the racket away," Rachel whispered to Alice and Kirsty.

"Actually, you *haven't* won," the umpire said. "You didn't play a full match, so there *is* no winner!" The goblin stared at him in disbelief.

"I *can't* play a full match because you disqualified everyone else!" he pointed out furiously.

The umpire shrugged. "Well, in that case, I will have to remain the keeper of the magic racket myself," he said smugly.

As Rachel watched the goblins arguing, an idea suddenly popped into her head. She turned to Kirsty and Alice. "Whatever I say, disagree with me!" she whispered. Then she rushed over to the umpire's chair.

Kirsty and Alice glanced at each other in excitement and confusion. Rachel obviously had a plan, but what could it be?

A Winning Return

"I think this goblin is right!" Rachel said loudly. "He's the only one left in the tournament, so he should be the keeper of the magic racket!"

The winning goblin looked a little surprised, but then he grinned. "She's right!" he agreed. "I won fair and square.

Hand over the racket!"

Kirsty smiled to herself. She guessed that Rachel was trying to distract the goblins by getting them to argue with one another.

"Don't let the goblins see you, Alice!" she whispered, hurrying over to the umpire.

"Well, I don't agree!" Kirsty said loudly, winking at Rachel. "It's very unfair that the other finalist was disqualified. I mean, he only threw his racket on the ground. He was ahead in the match. He's the real winner of Goblindon!"

"That's right!" the other finalist cried, darting back onto the court. "I'm a much better player. The racket should be mine!"

"No, it's mine!" the first goblin yelled.

"Actually, I thought it was unfair that the grunting goblin was disqualified, too," Rachel remarked. "Everyone grunts a little when they're playing sports."

"That's true," the grunting goblin shouted as he rushed up to the umpire. "I'm a magnificent player! That magic racket belongs to me!"

By now, all the goblins in the seats were rushing onto the court, yelling and complaining. Rachel and Kirsty grinned at each other.

"I was disqualified just because I had an orange headband!" grumbled one goblin.

"Yes, and you deserved it!" said another, frowning.

"Silence!" roared the umpire. "I'm in charge. What I say goes!"

"Your decisions are awful!" the "winning" goblin yelled. "You're nothing but a wishy-washy, selfish fool!"

The umpire looked furious. He jumped down from his chair, leaving the racket behind. He rushed over to the food cart

at the side of the court. Then he grabbed
a bowl of strawberries and cream and
dumped it over the other goblin's head.

"Help!" the
goblin shrieked
as cream ran
down his face.
The umpire
roared with
laughter.

"Alice, Rachel's plan
is working!" Kirsty whispered as the
goblins continued to argue with one
another. "Nobody's watching the magic
racket. Can you grab it now?"

Alice nodded and soared up toward
the umpire's chair. None of the goblins
noticed the tiny fairy as she fluttered
down and touched the magic racket.

Rachel and Kirsty watched as the racket immediately shrank to its Fairyland size, turning a deeper shade of pink as it did. Alice lifted up the racket and did a perfect backhand swing, smiling down at the girls in delight.

Kirsty grinned back. But then one of the goblins gave an angry shout.

"Look, a pesky fairy has the magic racket!" he yelled. "And I bet those awful girls helped her get it, too!" He pointed at Rachel and Kirsty.

The girls froze. Now what?

Game, Set, and Match

All of the goblins spun around and
glared at Rachel and Kirsty.

Feeling very nervous, the girls backed
away as the goblins stepped toward
them.

"Oh, help!" Rachel murmured
anxiously as she came to a stop. She had
come up against the fence at one end

of the court, next to the ball machine. "Kirsty, I think we might be trapped!"

Kirsty gulped as she stared at the crowd of angry goblins heading toward them. Frantically, she glanced across the court, hoping for an idea. Her gaze fell on the food cart.

"Alice!" Kirsty called to the tiny fairy who was hovering above the umpire's chair, looking worried. "Can you roll the cart over to us?"

Puzzled, Alice nodded and waved her
wand. Immediately, the cart sped over to
Rachel and Kirsty.

At once, Kirsty began grabbing bowls
of strawberries and cream from the cart
and pouring them into the ball machine.
Rachel saw what her friend was doing
and rushed to help. Meanwhile, the
goblins were getting closer every second.

"Here goes!" Kirsty cried when
all the bowls were empty.
She turned on the machine.

A second later,
a gooey, pink mess
of strawberries and
cream came shooting
out of the machine.
The goblins yelped
with surprise as
they were splashed
from head to toe
with the pink glop.

"I order you to stop!"
yelled the umpire goblin.
But his words were cut
short as a large blob
of strawberries

and cream flew straight into his
mouth. "Ugh!"
The umpire looked furious,
but then he suddenly
beamed with delight.
"Yum!" he said
happily. "That
tastes delicious!"
He began
slurping the
strawberries
and cream from
his hands and arms.
Rachel and Kirsty
both grinned as the
other goblins also began
to realize that the pink
mixture tasted good.

Eagerly, they scooped the strawberries
and cream off themselves and crammed
it into their mouths.

Soon the machine was empty, but the
goblins were full.

"Oh, I'm really stuffed now," groaned
the grunting goblin. "My tummy aches!"

"Mine, too," the other goblins
mumbled, holding their stomachs.

"It's time that you all went home," said Alice, smiling kindly at them. "You'll feel better soon."

The goblins nodded and staggered off, clutching their round tummies.

"Nice work, girls!" Alice said with a laugh, twirling happily in the air. "I thought we were in real trouble, until Kirsty had the brilliant idea of putting the strawberries and cream in the ball machine!"

"But it made a big mess!" Kirsty laughed, looking down at the squashed strawberries at their feet.

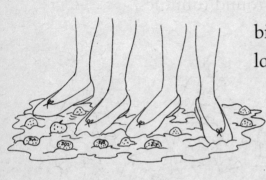

"I'll fix that," said Alice. She sent a swirl of fairy magic flying across the court, cleaning up the mess in an instant. "My magic put everything back in place inside the tennis club, too," Alice said, her eyes twinkling. "When the members come back, they'll never guess that there was a Goblindon tournament here!"

"Thanks, Alice," Rachel said.

"Now I need to hurry back to Fairyland and tell everyone the good news." Clutching her racket, Alice waved to Rachel and Kirsty. "Thank you for your help, girls. But don't forget, the Fairyland Olympics start soon, and one of the magic objects is still missing."

"We'll do our best to find it," Kirsty promised. Alice blew them a kiss and vanished in a burst of pink sparkles.

"That was a close call,"

Kirsty remarked, smiling at Rachel. "We really were outnumbered by goblins today, but we got Alice's racket back in the end."

"And we only have Gemma the Gymnastics Fairy's magic hoop left to find now," Rachel added. "Kirsty, we have to find it before the Fairyland Olympics start!"

"Definitely," Kirsty agreed, linking arms with her friend and grinning. "But maybe we'd better go home for lunch now. All those strawberries made me awfully hungry!"

Rachel and Kirsty need to help

Gemma

the Gymnastics Fairy!

Without Gemma's magic hoop, gymnastics
is being ruined for everyone. Can Rachel
and Kirsty help Gemma to get it back?

Join their next adventure
in this special sneak peek!

Someone in School

"Almost there," Rachel Walker said as she
and her best friend, Kirsty Tate, walked
along a sunny street. "Aunt Joan lives
around the corner, near my school."

"That's good," Kirsty said, glancing
down at the basket they were carrying.
"These chocolate Easter eggs might melt
if we had to go any farther!"

Kirsty was staying with Rachel's family

for spring break and the two girls were delivering Easter presents to Rachel's cousins.

"I can't believe it's Friday already," Rachel said. "The Fairyland Olympics start today!"

Kirsty nodded. "And we still haven't found Gemma the Gymnastics Fairy's magic hoop," she said. "If we don't get it back from the goblins soon, then all the gymnastics events at the Olympics will be spoiled."

The girls passed Tippington School, and Kirsty suddenly stopped. "That's strange," she said, staring across the playground. "I just saw some kids inside the school, dressed in green."

"School's closed for vacation," Rachel told

her. "And our uniforms are blue and gray, not green."

The same thought came to both girls at the same time, and they let out a gasp. "Goblins!" cried Rachel.

There's Magic in Every Series!

The Rainbow Fairies

The Weather Fairies

The Jewel Fairies

The Pet Fairies

The Fun Day Fairies

The Petal Fairies

The Dance Fairies

The Music Fairies

The Sports Fairies

The Party Fairies

Read them all!

SCHOLASTIC

www.scholastic.com

www.rainbowmagiconline.com

HIT entertainment

RMFAIRY2

THE PETAL FAIRIES

Keep Fairyland in Bloom!

SCHOLASTIC
www.scholastic.com
www.rainbowmagiconline.com

HIT entertainment

PFAIRIES